CARTOON NETWORK™

SCOOBY-DOO!™ AND THE
TRICK-OR-TREAT THIEF

By Jesse Leon McCann

WB™

SCHOLASTIC INC.

**New York   Toronto   London   Auckland   Sydney
Mexico City   New Delhi   Hong Kong   Buenos Aires**

For my son, Jesse Blake McCann, who is of good heart and honorable nature; of whom I am very proud.

Cover design by Carisa Swenson
Interior design by Bethany Dixon

12 11 10 9 8 7 6   4 5 6 7/0
Special thanks to Duendes del Sur for cover and interior illustrations.
Printed in the U.S.A.
First Scholastic printing, September 2002

Scooby-Doo and his pals from Mystery, Inc. were very excited. It was Halloween night and they were looking forward to passing out goodies to trick-or-treaters.

"Scooby-BOO! Ree-hee-hee!" Scooby laughed.

"Like, real funny, Scoob! You almost scared me." Shaggy licked his lips hungrily. "Now, let's see if we can't scare up something to eat!"

"Oh, no you don't," warned Daphne as she waved Shaggy and Scooby away from the treats. "Those are for the trick-or-treaters, and they'll be here soon."

The gang anxiously waited for the doorbell to ring. Several minutes passed. Then several more. But no trick-or-treaters came to the door. The gang peeked outside. There wasn't a kid in costume in sight.

"That's strange," said Velma, frowning. "It's certainly late enough for trick-or-treating!"

"There's something unusual going on here," Fred decided. "Come on, gang! Let's go see if we can get to the bottom of this."

It was quiet outside. And it was spooky. In fact, it was spooky because it was so quiet.

"Where do you think everyone is?" Velma asked.

"Like, maybe they were abducted by weird aliens with throbbing brains and huge eyeballs!" Shaggy suggested.

"R-r-ruge r-r-ryeballs?" Scooby gulped. "Roh, no!"

"Relax, you two. I'm sure there's a perfectly reasonable explanation." Daphne pointed to a nearby treehouse. "Look! There's some kids over there!"

Inside the treehouse, the gang discovered why hardly anyone was out on Halloween night. Somebody . . . a sneaky thief . . . was going around stealing everyone's trick-or-treats!

"I was minding my own business," explained a little girl in a cowgirl costume. "Then, all of a sudden, this mysterious hombre cut me off at the pass. He rustled away my treats and disappeared into the night."

"Jinkies!" cried Velma. "That's terrible!"

"I was slipping from house to house, as stealthy as a mouse, when out of nowhere the thief appeared," reported a boy dressed as a spy. "When he saw what I was carrying, he grabbed it and gave me the slip!"

A boy in a clown costume told a similar story, ending with the thief taking his bag of goodies. The Mystery, Inc. gang looked at one another. This thief was good . . . <u>too</u> good!

"Like, what a rotten thing to do!" Shaggy muttered.

"Reah!" Scooby scowled.

"We're afraid to do any more trick-or-treating with the thief on the loose," sighed the clown. "If we got more treats, he'd just steal those, too."

These kids weren't the only ones visited by the thief. Almost every child in the neighborhood had lost their treats!

"This sure is fishy! Halloween goodies aren't bait for thieves!" exclaimed a boy dressed as a deep-sea diver. "But that thief snagged mine hook, line, and sinker!"

All the kids from the neighborhood told their own story. In each case, the thief came up with a new way to take their goodies, then disappeared.

"Jeepers," Daphne commented. "This thief sounds almost supernatural!"

"Zoinks!" cried Shaggy. "A thief with supernatural powers to steal snacks! Like, suddenly bug-eyed aliens don't sound so bad!"

"Not supernatural, just very clever," Fred said. "Don't worry, kids! We'll solve this mystery <u>and</u> get your treats back!"

Daphne frowned. "Who would be mean enough to ruin Halloween for a bunch of kids?"

"Somebody with the skill to move through shadows without been seen," Velma explained. "In fact, he could be watching us this very moment."

"Rulp!" Scooby shivered. He had the feeling Velma was right!

"Let's see if the grownups in the neighborhood saw anything." Fred walked up to a house. "We might be able to get some clues about this thief . . ."

Scooby and Shaggy ran ahead of Fred and rang the doorbell. They thought they might as well do a little trick-or-treating while they were there.

"What do you want?!" said the woman who jerked open the door. "Can't you see I'm trying to watch my shows? I don't like Halloween and I don't like trick-or-treaters! Now, go away!"

Next the gang came upon the local dentist.

"I hope you kids aren't going to eat a lot of goodies tonight!" he scolded them. "Sugar is a tooth's worst nightmare!"

"Don't worry, doctor," Daphne smiled. "We always brush after every meal."

"Hrmm! Even you?" Dr. Lockjaw pointed a stern finger at Scooby.

"Reah! Reah!" Scooby smiled a big grin. His teeth were sparkly white. "Ree?"

This seemed to make the dentist happy. "Very well, then. I can't stick around. I must get home to give out my Halloween treats — apples and dental floss . . . !"

"Like, whew! That doc sure is strict!" Shaggy sighed. "But I don't think he's so ungroovy that he'd want to ruin Halloween for the kids."

Next they came to the Moneybucket mansion. Mrs. Moneybucket had the finest Halloween decorations and gave out the best treats in the neighborhood.

On this Halloween night, however, she didn't seem very festive.

"It's terrible! Terrible!" Mrs. Moneybucket cried. "Someone has stolen my priceless red ruby while I was giving out goodies to trick-or-treaters! Who would do such a thing?"

Mrs. Moneybucket's faithful butler Hudson was looking everywhere for the jewel. The gang could tell that the ruby was nowhere to be found in the mansion.

Mrs. Moneybucket became so upset, she couldn't talk. Hudson the butler explained what had happened.

"I-It was quite extraordinary!" Hudson stammered. "While the madam dispensed sweetened treats as she does every All Hallow's Eve, I went about my duties. As I dusted the mantelpiece in the foyer, I was shocked to see a thief grabbing madam's favorite ruby. In a blink, the scoundrel was gone!"

"Oh, boo-hoo-hoo!" wailed Mrs. Moneybucket in despair. "Hudson, whatever shall I do?"

The gang was quite puzzled as they left the Moneybucket mansion.

"Jinkies!" Velma exclaimed. "A thief who steals trick or treats <u>and</u> precious gems?"

"We've got to stop that thief," Fred declared. "But first we're going back to our place to get some things."

"Pizzas?" asked Shaggy hopefully.

"Rilkshakes?" guessed Scooby.

"No," Fred smiled. "Halloween costumes!"

Soon Fred and the others were back on the street in costumes.

"Heads up, gang!" Fred warned them. "I think I see someone lurking in the bushes up ahead!"

Shaggy and Scooby-Doo gulped nervously.

"Just keep walking," Velma whispered. "We're almost upon him."

The gang walked past the bushes, anxiously waiting for the thief to jump out. Fred had a rope in his pocket, ready to lasso the robber.

But the Mystery, Inc. kids passed the bushes and the thief <u>didn't</u> jump out! In fact, after they went by, the thief sneaked away toward some other unsuspecting kids in the distance.

"That's strange," Fred remarked. "He left us alone. It's almost as if the thief recognized us and knew it was a trap!"

"We'll have to try again," Velma said. "This time, we'll make sure the thief doesn't recognize anyone. In fact, we'll disguise Shaggy and Scooby so well, even we wouldn't know them!"

"Like, no way, Velma!" Shaggy complained. "Scooby and I have had enough thief hunting for one night. That guy is too sneaky and creepy."

Velma reached into her treat sack and pulled something out. "Would you do it for a few Scooby Snacks?"

Everyone knew the answer to that question. Soon Scooby and Shaggy were in new costumes, pretending to trick-or-treat.

"Oh, look at us!" Shaggy called out in a high-pitched girl's voice. "We're just two poor, little ragamuffins out trick-or-treating by ourselves with big sacks of goodies. I do hope no one tries to take them!"

"Ree-hee-hee!" Scooby laughed at Shaggy's hammy acting.

"Jeepers, talk about bad performances," Daphne joked. She was hiding nearby with Velma and Fred. "I just hope those boys don't frighten the thief away. They're scarier than he is!"

When Shaggy and Scooby wandered past, the thief jumped out. He tried to grab their trick-or-treat sack. At almost the same time, Fred, Velma, and Daphne jumped out of their hiding place, too.

"Ah ha!" shouted the thief.

"Gotcha!" hollered Fred.

"Zoinks!" yelled Shaggy.

Scooby and Shaggy were so frightened, they ran away! They knocked their friends aside, which allowed the thief to escape in the opposite direction.

"Shaggy! Scooby! Come back!" Daphne called. "The thief isn't chasing you."

"Just the opposite," Fred frowned. "He's getting away."

"That's okay," Velma smiled. "I think I know a way to follow that sneaky thief!"

Velma was right. Although the thief had disappeared into the night, he had sprung a leak in one of his stolen sacks. He was leaving a trick-or-treat trail for the gang to follow!

The trail led them into a deserted field nearby. In the middle of the field was a dark, spooky shack.

The kids crept quietly but quickly up to the shack. Daphne shined her flashlight into the dusty gloom. Inside were all the trick-or-treat sacks that had been stolen that night.

"This is the thief's hideout, all right," Velma said. "Let's go in and get those treats."

"I say we get them back to the kids as soon as possible." Daphne turned the rusty knob and opened the shack's creaky door.

"And, like, I say we call the police," Shaggy replied. "Because I'm not going in! The thief might still be in there!"

"Reah! And riders!" Scooby said, eyeing their spooky surroundings.

"Spiders? Don't be silly!" Daphne smiled. "We can't let that stop us from saving Halloween, can we?"

Inside, it looked like the treats of every kid in town were in that shack!

"That's odd," Velma pointed. "Every sack has a tag with a child's name on it. Why would the thief go through the trouble to label them?"

Fred inspected some candy on a rickety table. "It looks like the thief was going through these treats, looking for something. I wonder what?"

As the gang continued their investigation, they didn't realize that someone was outside at the window, watching them!

Meanwhile, the thief leaped inside through a big hole in the ceiling. "Ah ha!" he bellowed.

The Mystery, Inc. gang was so scared, they raced out the door!

"Like, I knew it!" Shaggy cried as he and Scooby led the retreat. "That's no thief! That's a ghost!"

"A rhost?! Roh no!" Scooby yelped, and ran even faster.

When the gang was a safe distance away, they discussed the situation.

"That was no ghost," Velma said firmly. "He just sneaked up on us and caught us by surprise."

"And that's exactly what we've got to do to him," Fred said. "Come on, gang. I've got an idea!"

Fred took the others to the local community theater, where he worked part-time. They loaded a bunch of set pieces, props, and costumes into the back of the Mystery Machine. All the items they borrowed were used by the theater to put on plays.

COMMUNITY THEATER

BEAR COSTUME

A short time later, Shaggy and Scooby were dressed as bears. They stood in front of a house that hadn't been there an hour before.

"Man, do I feel silly!" Shaggy complained. "Like, what are we supposed to do now?"

"Pretend to be trick-or-treating!" Fred called from behind the house.

Shaggy knocked on the door of the house. Daphne pleasantly opened the door from inside and gave Shaggy and Scooby some treats. Then Shaggy pretended to be really surprised and pulled a red cherry candy out of his sack.

"Like, look Scooby!" Shaggy exclaimed loudly. "That nice lady just gave me a big ruby!"

As if on cue, the thief jumped out when he heard Shaggy mention the ruby.

"Ah ha!" boomed the thief, pointing at Shaggy and Scooby.

"Zoinks," said Shaggy in a wee voice.

"Reah, roinks," added Scooby with a squeak.

The thief approached them swiftly. He slunk closer and closer. He reached out his hands. And then, just as he was about to pounce . . .

"Now!" cried Fred.

Suddenly the house came apart as ropes were tugged, pulleys were pulled, and a net was yanked. As the walls went down, the thief went up!

It was all a trap that Fred had devised. Using sets and props from the community theater, they built a phony house good enough to fool anyone. The thief had fallen for it!

"Good job, everyone!" Fred exclaimed proudly. "Now, let's see who this villain really is!"

"Like, yeah!" nodded Shaggy. "Let's take a look at the guy who is so low, so mean, he would steal from kids on Halloween! Who is this creepy thief?"

"Reah! Roo? Roo?" snorted Scooby-Doo.

"Hudson?!" said the gang all at once.

"Oh, dear!" Hudson said meekly. "Madam is going to be <u>so</u> cross with me."

"Man, I don't believe it!" Shaggy laughed as he took candy from his pocket and put it into his mouth. "Like, the <u>butler</u> did it! I've been waiting years to say that!"

Shaggy bit down hard on the candy.

"Yeowch!"

It wasn't candy! It was a bright red ruby!

"Madam's ruby!" Hudson exclaimed. "Oh, I'm so relieved!"

Hudson was quite ashamed as he explained why he became the thief. When he was dusting, he accidentally knocked Mrs. Moneybucket's ruby into someone's trick-or-treat sack. Only he didn't know whose. So he stole all the treat sacks, hoping to recover the lost gem. He made sure he tagged each sack with the child's name so he could return them later.

"I'm so terribly sorry," fretted Hudson. "I didn't mean to cause all this trouble."

"Well, I guess you can be forgiven." Velma smiled. "But next time you should admit you made a mistake and ask for help. You'll find telling the truth a lot easier."

"Yes, miss," Hudson nodded. "Believe me, I've learned a valuable lesson."

The Mystery, Inc. gang helped Hudson return all the treats to their rightful owners. Mrs. Moneybucket was so happy to see her ruby again, she didn't even ask where it had gone to.

"It looks like everyone is having a happy Halloween, after all!" Daphne smiled.

"Like, you can say that again!" Shaggy grinned. "Now me and Scoob have some trick-or-treating of our own to do! Right, Scooby?"

"Scooby-Dooby-Doo!" cheered Scooby.